Story Soup

Written by **Abie Longstaff** ★ Illustrated by Nila Aye

Ollie was mixing a story.

He stirred the soup pot and added . . .

Th...

For Harry, Lottie and Sophie.

A. L.

For Ethan and Ella, two of the most original and creative Story Soupers I know.

Thank you for being the perfect inspiration.

N. A.

. . . a skateboard.

The mixture churned and foamed.

Roll

Flump

Bing

Chungle

Bubble

Whirr

Whoosh!

A story shot out!

ONCE UPON A TIME... there was a brave skateboard...

The kitchen door burst open and Ollie's sister Susie came running in.
"A story!" she cried. "Can I put something in?"
"Nope," said Ollie. "This story is only going to be about skateboards."

"Huh?" said Ollie. "What's that princess doing in there?"
He leaned over the soup pot and . . .

. . . blew.

All of a sudden there was a gust of wind!

"What an exciting beginning," said Susie.
"I love our story already."
"It's not OUR story," said Ollie.
"It's MY story."

Susie chucked in a pirate.

"Stop adding things!"
Ollie cried.

Captain Barnacle fished Adelina
out of the water . . .

. . . and locked her in the hold.
"Why have you shut me in here?" she wept.
"I'm the baddie," explained Barnacle.
"I'm supposed to be mean."

"And now he's locked up the skateboard," complained Ollie. "Hmm. Maybe he's mean because he's hungry?"

Ollie tossed him a banana.
Susie threw in a bottle of ketchup.

"Mmm," chomped the captain. "I love yellow sausages."

"That pirate character is far too silly," groaned Ollie, as he mixed in a purse. "Now Adelina can buy her freedom."

Whiskers yawned.
Flick went her tail and into the soup pot fell a jar of honey.

Susie giggled and stirred the story. "I can't wait to see what happens next," she said.

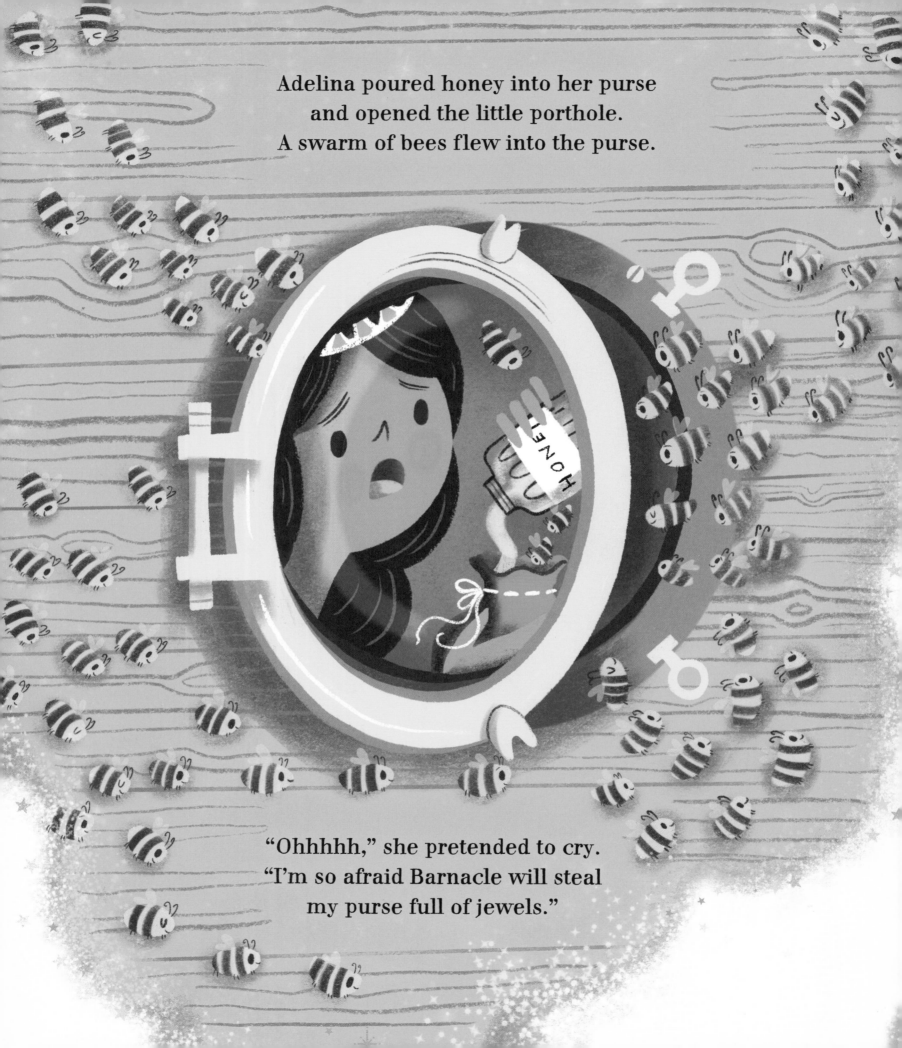

Adelina poured honey into her purse
and opened the little porthole.
A swarm of bees flew into the purse.

"Ohhhhh," she pretended to cry.
"I'm so afraid Barnacle will steal
my purse full of jewels."

"Surely he's not going to fall for that trick?" whispered Ollie.

"Well, he IS silly," Susie whispered back.

Barnacle chuckled evilly and unlocked the hold. He opened the purse and . . .

ZZZZZZZZZZZZZZZZZZZZZ

. . . a cloud of bees flew out!

"Arghhh!" he cried
and jumped into the water.

Adelina leapt onto the skateboard
and skated across the deck.

Susie threw a pony into the pot.
"No more random things!" Ollie cried, sweeping his hand to the side and accidentally knocking in a set of teeth.

Suddenly a vampire pony galloped across the deck. He gnashed his teeth and

CRUNCH!

He bit the skateboard in half.

Ollie was furious. "See what you did!" he said.
"You spoiled my skateboarding story."
"I didn't," said Susie. "It's much more interesting now."
She stuck out her tongue and started throwing in anything she could find.

Ollie stamped his foot.
"STOP IT! It's MY story!" he yelled.

Susie took one side of the pot.

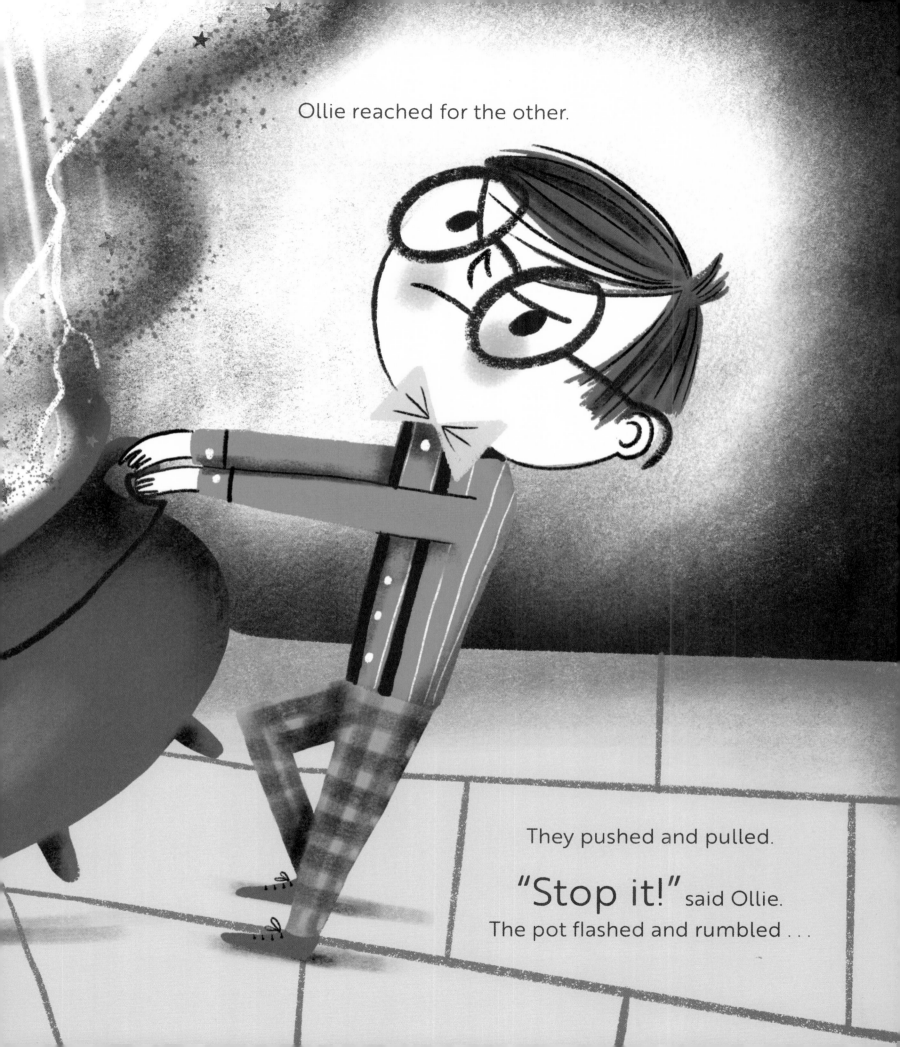

Ollie reached for the other.

They pushed and pulled.

"Stop it!" said Ollie.
The pot flashed and rumbled . . .

A mighty storm broke
the ship in two.

Ollie looked at his sister.
"We have to save them all!"
Susie pointed at a butter dish.
"Help me reach this," she said.

Together they lifted it down
and threw it into the pot.

Adelina pulled herself onto the dish
and the vampire pony clattered on after her.
"Here!" cried Adelina.
She held out her hand to help Barnacle.

"I'm sorry I locked you up," said Barnacle.
"I'm sick of being a baddie. Now I want to be good."
"You could help me fix the ship," suggested Adelina.
'That would be good."
"I will," said Barnacle.
"But first, where are my yellow sausages?"

Together they made the best ship in the world,
with a cardboard slide, a tinfoil sail, egg-beater propellers,
shiny wings and a wonderful skateboard ramp.

"Is this the end?" asked Ollie.
"It doesn't have to be," said Susie.
"I guess you could help for a bit longer," said Ollie.
Together they stirred the mix.

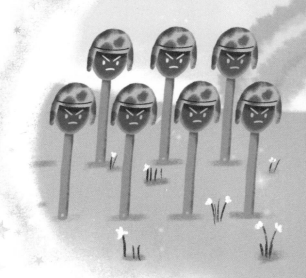

"Now we've saved each other,
let's go save the world," said Adelina.
"Neigh!" said the pony, gnashing
its teeth happily.

So off they flew!

Together, they defeated sea-snake cats . . .

. . . saved a rainbow zebra from an army of wooden spoons . . .

. . . and found a chest of enormous jewels.

Which all goes to show that,

IF YOU
CO-OPERATE,
YOU CAN
ACCOMPLISH
ANYTHING.

"Oi!" said Ollie,
"I didn't ask for a moral!"

A faraway king heard of their achievements.
He held an enormous ball in their honour.
Every prince wanted to marry Adelina.
Every princess wanted to ride the vampire pony.
And every chef wanted to cook yellow sausages.

*Stay forever!
You will be rich
and famous and
popular!*

But the three friends linked arms (and tail), danced back to the ship and soared off into the sunset in search of more adventures.

What a soppy ending!

Well, you know how it always ends . . .

AND THEY ALL

VED HAPPILY EVER AFTER . . .

"That was a great story," sighed Susie.
"The best ever," said Ollie. "Let's mix another one tomorrow."

★ STORY SOUP RECIPE ★

EQUIPMENT:
- Story Soup pot (e.g. a washing-up bowl, cardboard box, or anything!)
- Spoon for stirring
- Imagination

METHOD:

1. Stir in an ingredient of your choice (Sock? Teddy? Jam jar? Hairbrush?)

This is your hero. What's their name? Where are they going?

2. Mix in something shiny.

This is the hero's favourite toy, and it has a special power. What can it do?

3. Whisk in the weirdest ingredient you can find.

Uh oh! That ingredient was rotten. It's your villain, and it wants the toy! Why?

4. Sprinkle in the closest three things to you.

Oops. The baddie is using these to steal the toy . . . and they're winning!

Quick, help! Shake the pot to swap everyone's items around. Who gets what?

5. Throw in something natural for seasoning.

This ingredient has a secret power. Who will use it, and will they win?

Happily Ever After? That's up to you.

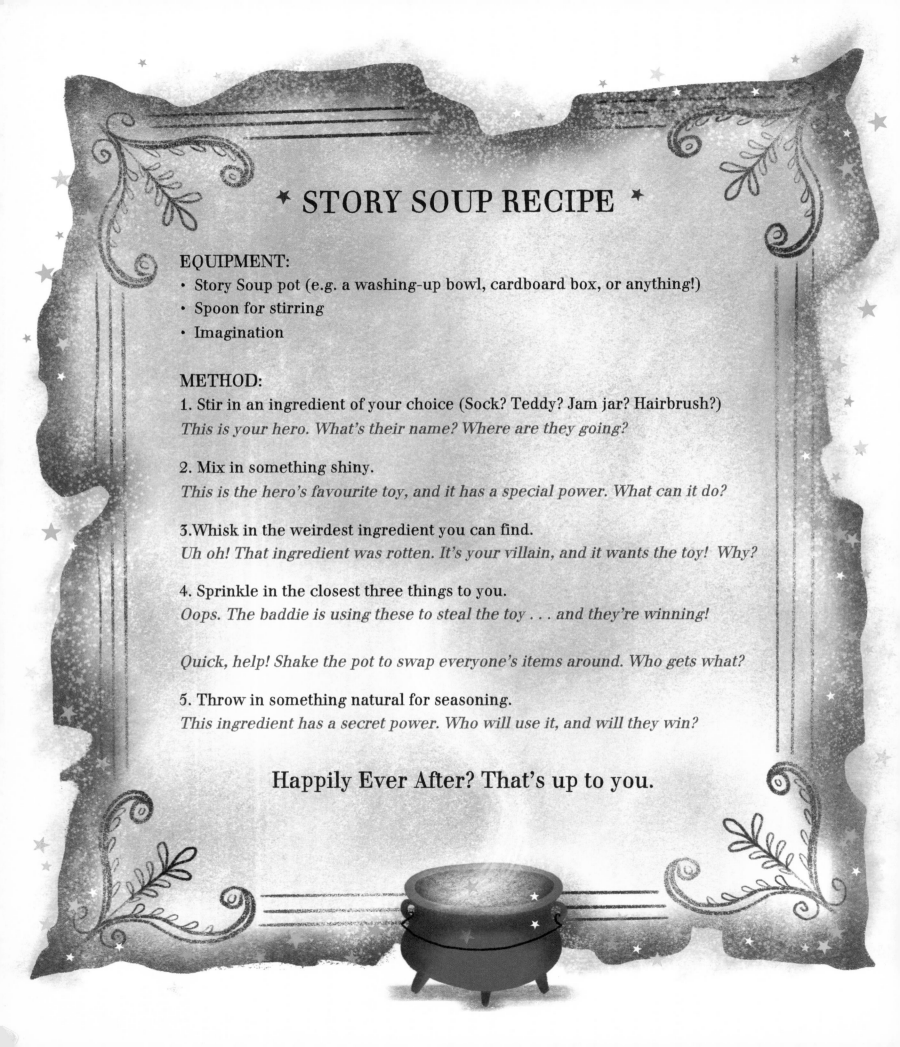

Bing

Chungle

Bubble

Flump